HOW to FIND an ELEPHANT

Kate Banks

Pictures by Boris Kulikov

MARGARET FERGUSON BOOKS

Farrar Straus Giroux
New York

Farrar Straus Giroux Books for Young Readers
An imprint of Macmillan Publishing Group, LLC
175 Fifth Avenue, New York 10010

Text copyright © 2017 by Kate Banks
Pictures copyright © 2017 by Boris Kulikov
All rights reserved
Color separations by Bright Arts (H.K.) Ltd.
Printed in China by RR Donnelley Asia Printing Solutions Ltd.,
Dongguan City, Guangdong Province
Designed by Roberta Pressel
First edition, 2017
1   3   5   7   9   10   8   6   4   2

mackids.com

Library of Congress Cataloging-in-Publication Data

Names: Banks, Kate, 1960– author. | Kulikov, Boris, 1966– illustrator.
Title: How to find an elephant / Kate Banks ; pictures by Boris Kulikov.
Description: First edition. | New York : Farrar Straus Giroux, 2017. |
    "Margaret Ferguson Books." | Summary: A boy provides instructions
    as he searches high and low for an elephant, which the reader can
    find in the illustrations.
Identifiers: LCCN 2017001864 | ISBN 9780374335083 (hardcover)
Subjects: | CYAC: Adventure and adventurers—Fiction. | Elephants—Fiction.
Classification: LCC PZ7.B22594 HI 2017 | DDC [E]—dc23
LC record available at https://lccn.loc.gov/2017001864

Our books may be purchased in bulk for promotional, educational, or business use.
Please contact your local bookseller or the Macmillan Corporate and Premium
Sales Department at (800) 221-7945 ext. 5442 or by e-mail
at MacmillanSpecialMarkets@macmillan.com.

For Boris. Thank you.
—K.B.

For Max, Andre, and Yelena.
—B.K.

The best time to look for an elephant is on a dull day
when clouds hover on the horizon
looking like spaceships.
And you're thinking up something to do.

The best place to find an elephant is in the wild.

You will need to pack some food and a pair of binoculars.

You may want to take a flute.

And bring a blanket—

one that's tasseled and brightly colored,

with a story woven through the cloth to tell the elephant.

The first thing you will want to do is climb to the
top of the nearest tree.
Take out your binoculars and look for something
large and gray.

If you don't see an elephant,
then you will have to go into the jungle.

Keep an eye out for elephant footprints.
They look like this.
But don't expect to hear the elephant's footsteps,
because elephants walk on tiptoe.

When you get thirsty, stop at a watering hole for a drink.
While you are there, you can take a dip.

And don't forget that elephants are fine swimmers.

If you come to a house, knock on the door and politely say,
"Has anyone seen an elephant?"
And if no one has, then go deeper into the jungle.

It may start to rain, but you can take shelter under a large leaf.
While you wait out the storm, play a tune on your flute.

You are bound to be hungry. So find a soft, shady spot
and have your lunch.
In case an elephant decides to join you, gather some
bamboo shoots and tree bark for the elephant to eat.
You will need plenty, because elephants have big appetites.
No pizza or chips, please.

At some point you will probably bump into a chimpanzee.
If you are feeling brave, ask if you can swing on its vine.

Be sure to jump off when you see an eagle's nest.
And ask the eagle to carry you over the trees to
the edge of the jungle.

When you get there, take a good look around.
And if you happen to spot something big and
gray, tiptoe closer.
You'll want to see if it's an elephant or not.
If it's not an elephant, then you'll just have to
keep looking.

And if you begin to feel tired, go to the
top of a hill that has long, lush grass
swaying in the breeze
and some crickets to sing you to sleep.
Spread out your blanket and lie down.
Remind yourself to have sweet dreams
of elephants.

If you should be wakened by the ground shaking . . .

. . . and find yourself wrapped in a hug and lifted toward the sky,
then you will know that an elephant has found you!